S0-DLE-984

Mr. Mombo's
BALLOON FLIGHT
Written by Fiona Conboy
Illustrated by Stephen Holmes

CAN YOU SEE?
Mr. Mombo's parrot hiding
somewhere in the picture?

SETTING OFF

Mr. Mombo, the famous balloon explorer, and his excited crew, Timothy, Max the dog, and Mr. Mombo's parrot, are setting off on an amazing round-the-world adventure. They plan to visit the North Pole, the African desert, the South American jungle, and even the Australian bush! As they float up, up, and away they can see people waving good-bye. "Those fishermen look like tiny specks in their little fishing boats," laughs Timothy. "Can you see the dolphins, Timmy?" asks Mr. Mombo, as Timothy peers down over the edge of the basket.

Bon voyage, Mr. Mombo!

How many people can you see fishing?

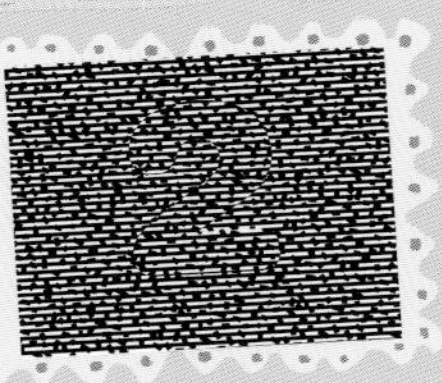

How many people are waving from the shore?

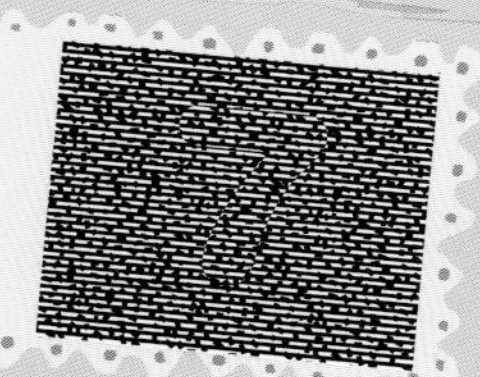

Can you count the dolphins?

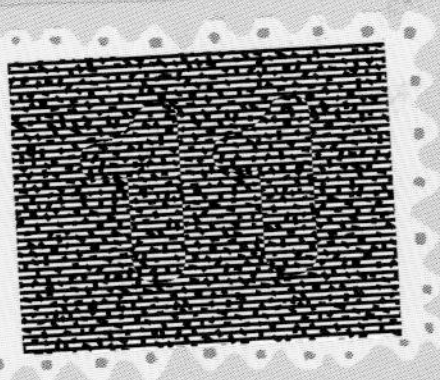

Black-faced seagulls fly around the balloon. Can you count them?

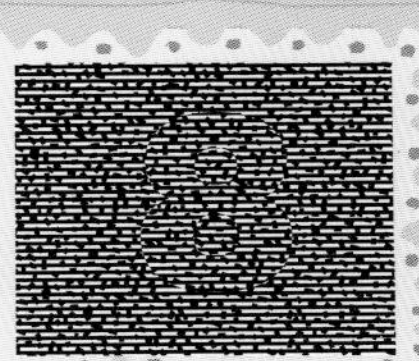

Mr. Mombo has brought some useful things with him.

CAN YOU SEE?

a wrench, a guidebook, a pair of sunglasses, a screwdriver, a handkerchief, and a magnifying glass?

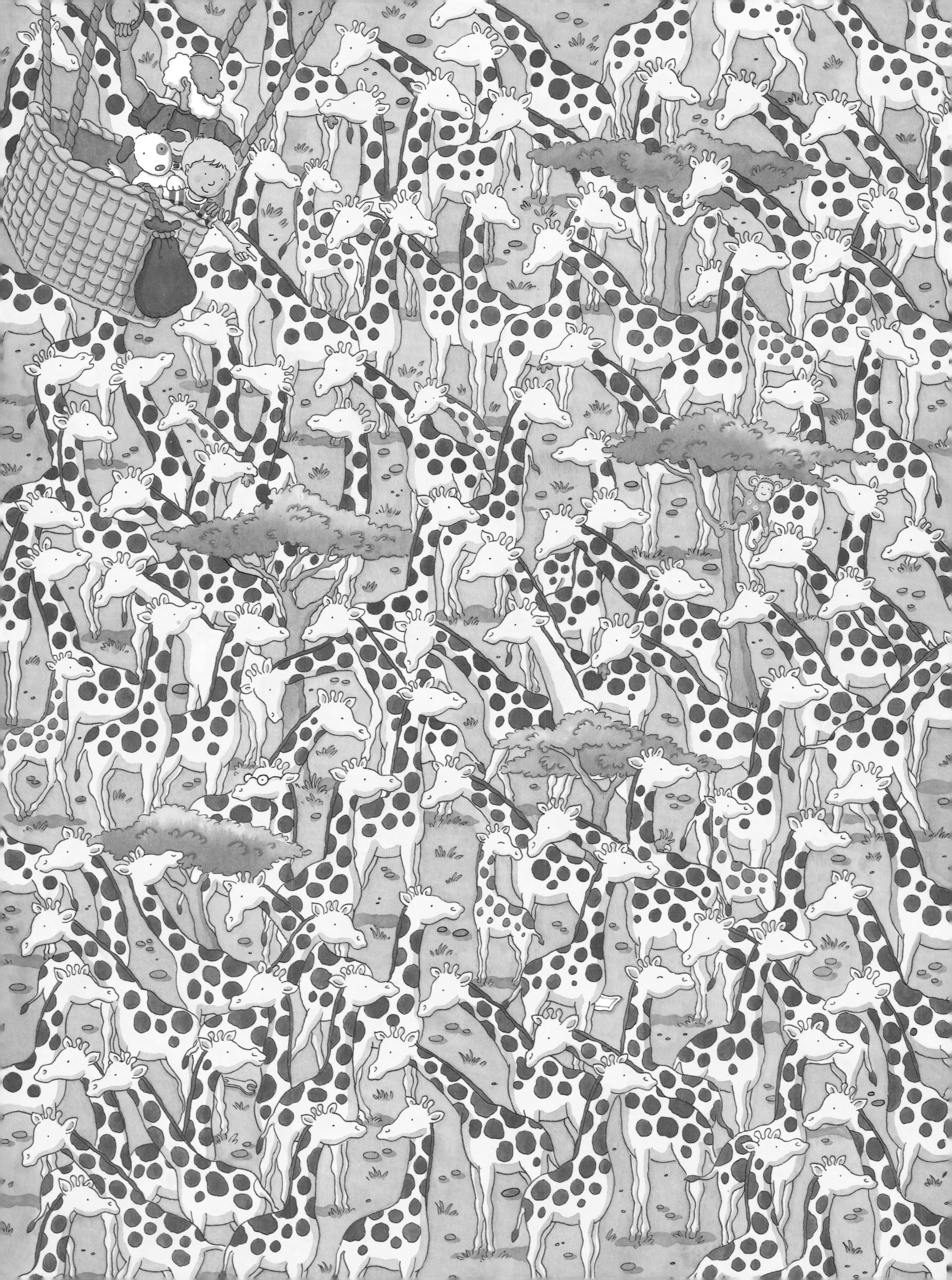

AFRICA

Today Mr. Mombo is flying over a country in Africa. It is very hot and dry—Timothy wishes they had cold drinks and ice cream on board! Soon they see a big herd of giraffes roaming on a grassy plain.

"Look at all those spots!" Timothy cries. Mr. Mombo lets the balloon drop down very low so they can get a good look at the animals. They see a few interesting things as they pass over.

If you look carefully, you will see them too.

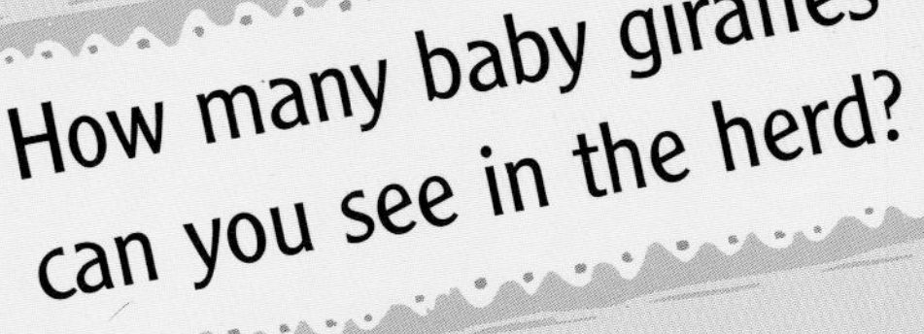

How many baby giraffes can you see in the herd?

Can you count the giraffes eating leaves?

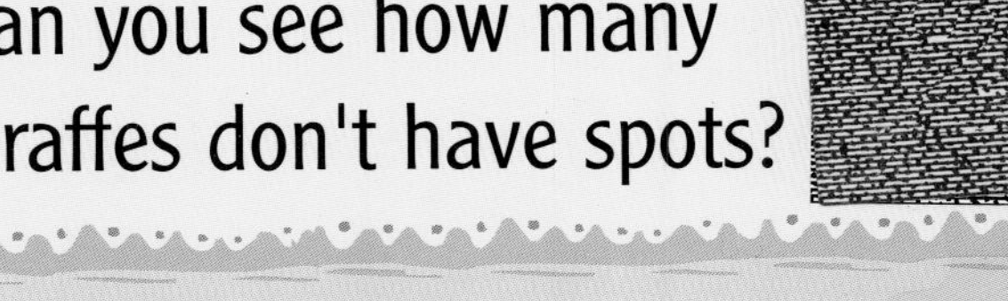

Can you see how many giraffes don't have spots?

Trees shade the animals from the sun. Can you count them?

CAN YOU SEE?

In one of the trees there is an animal that isn't a giraffe. Can you see her?

Can you see Mr. Mombo's parrot?

Mr. Mombo has lost his wrench. Can you see it?

One of the giraffes is wearing glasses! Can you see him?

Mr. Mombo has dropped his handkerchief. Can you see where it landed?

ARCTIC

Mr. Mombo has flown north to the Arctic. It is much colder here, so Mr. Mombo and his crew have put on their warmest woolly clothes. Beneath the balloon they can see a large group of animals lazing on the ice. "Look at all the seals, Timmy," says Mr. Mombo. "Some of them have young pups!" Timothy sees some unusual objects lying among the seals.

Can you see them, too?

How many baby seals can you see?

How many seals don't have spots?

How many seals are in the water?

How many seals are carrying or eating fish?

CAN YOU SEE?

There is a walrus among the seals. Can you see her?

Can you see the polar bear?

Where is Mr. Mombo's parrot?

Can you find the seal wearing headphones?

Mr. Mombo has dropped his glove. Can you find it?

From the cold winds of the Arctic, Mr. Mombo has flown south to the plains of North America, where the sun is beating down on a herd of buffaloes roaming on the prairie. "Buffaloes love to 'bathe' in dust," says Mr. Mombo. "That's why some of them look very dirty!" Timothy thinks the big furry beasts look very frightening with their big humps and sharp horns. He is glad to be up in the sky in Mr. Mombo's balloon!

How many buffaloes are sleeping?

How many baby buffaloes can you see?

Some of the buffaloes don't have horns. Can you count them?

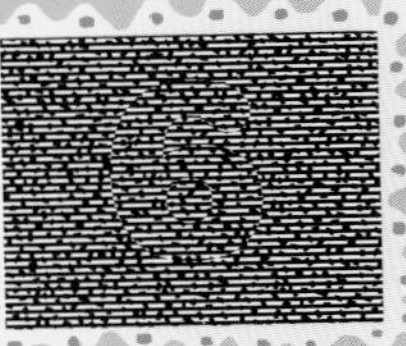

Can you see how many dusty buffaloes there are?

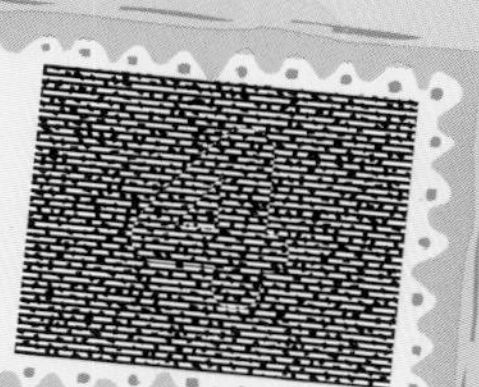

One buffalo is wearing a bell.
Can you see her?

Where is Mr. Mombo's parrot?

There are two rabbits in the picture.
Can you see them?

Can you find two buffaloes
fighting with each other?

Mr. Mombo has lost his magnifying glass.
Can you find it?

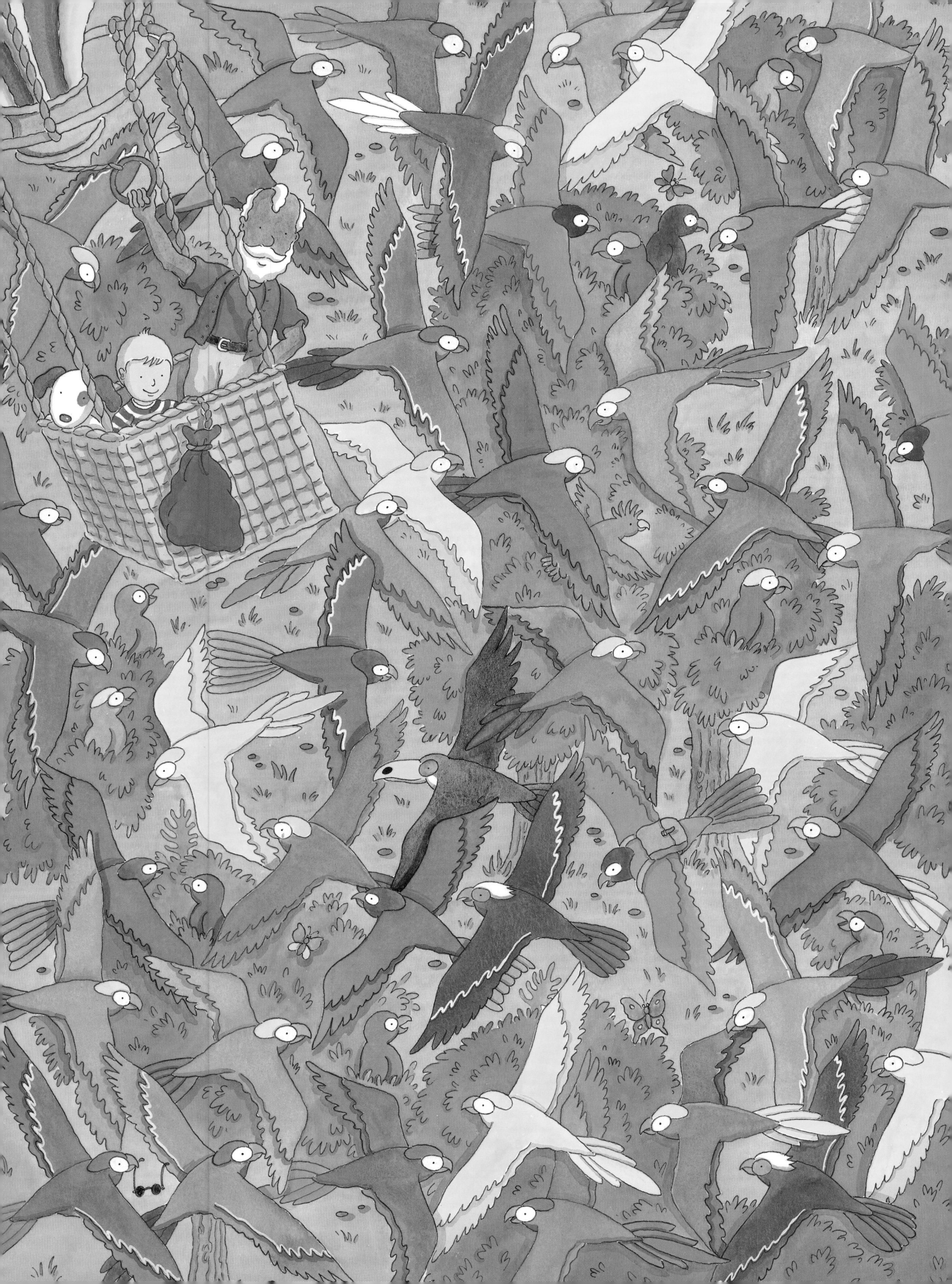

SOUTH AMERICA

Mr. Mombo has arrived in South America and is flying over an Amazonian jungle. "Look at all the brightly colored birds," says Timothy, pointing down at the flock of multicolored parrots flying around them. The parrots squawk noisily as the balloon brushes the leaves of the jungle trees. "We'd better make sure our parrot doesn't stay behind with them!" says Mr. Mombo.

Can you see how many parrots are resting in the trees?

How many toucans can you find in the picture?

How many yellow parrots can you see?

Some parrots have orange tails. Can you count them?

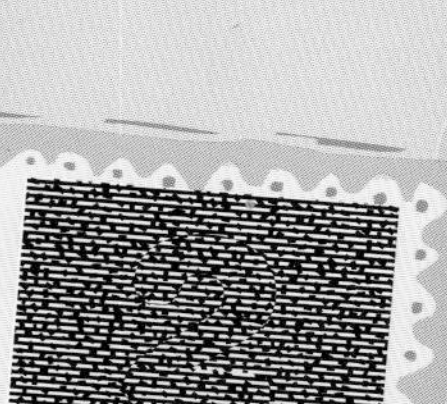

Where is Mr. Mombo's parrot?

Can you see the three butterflies?

Mr. Mombo has lost his sunglasses. Can you see them?

One of the parrots is carrying a backpack. Can you find her?

Can you see the white-tailed parrot?

AUSTRALIA

"G'day, Australia!" shouts Mr. Mombo as they reach the land of kangaroos and
koalas. Timothy laughs as he watches a herd of kangaroos hopping around.
"They can't walk—they can only hop or jump,"
Mr. Mombo explains. "And they use their long tails to balance."
"Why do some of the kangaroos have pockets?" asks Timothy.
"They are mother kangaroos carrying their babies, or joeys,
in a pouch," smiles Mr. Mombo. "It looks cozy, doesn't it!"

How many kangaroos are carrying their joeys?

How many gray kangaroos can you see?

Some kangaroos are wearing sunglasses. Can you count them?

Can you see how many big gray rocks there are?

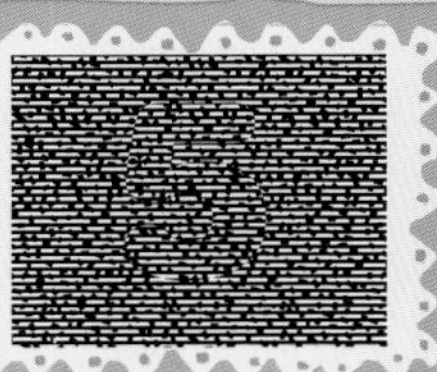

CAN YOU SEE?

Can you find the snake?

Where is Mr. Mombo's parrot?

There is a koala among the kangaroos. Can you see him?

Find the kangaroo wearing a hat.

Can you see the kangaroo waving at you?

ASIA

From Australia, Mr. Mombo has flown his balloon west to India, home of the largest member of the cat family, the tiger. Timothy hears one tiger let out a loud roar and looks down through his binoculars.

"Look at those sharp teeth!" he gasps.

"I wish I could go for a swim in that water," says Mr. Mombo. "But I don't think the tigers would make me very welcome!"

Look closely at the scene, and you might be able to see some strange things happening!

Some of the tigers don't have stripes. How many?

How many trees have brown trunks?

How many tigers have their paws in the river?

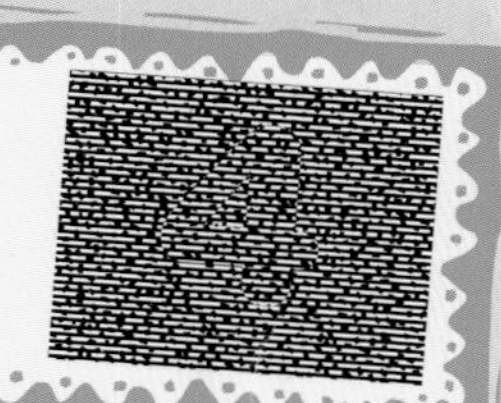

How many tigers are roaring?

CAN YOU SEE?

Can you find the tiger climbing up a tree?

Where is Mr. Mombo's parrot?

One of the tigers has stripes going the wrong way! Can you see him?

Mr. Mombo has dropped his boot.
Can you find it?

Can you see the lizard?

ANTARCTIC

Mr. Mombo has made his last journey south and has finally arrived in Antarctica, the South Pole.
"Time to put on your winter clothes again, Timmy," he says.
"Look at the penguins. They look like waiters!" laughs Timothy as he watches the penguins waddling around on the ice.
"I wouldn't swim in that water."
"They are used to the cold temperatures," explains Mr. Mombo.

Look carefully at the penguins, and you will see some unusual objects among them!

How many baby penguins can you count?

How many penguins have caught fish?

How many penguins are lying on their bellies?

Some penguins have red beaks. Can you count them?

CAN YOU SEE?

One of the penguins has an egg. Can you find her?

Can you find the penguin with a cane?

There are two penguins in the water. Can you see them?

Where is Mr. Mombo's parrot?

Mr. Mombo can't find his screwdriver. Can you see it?

MIDDLE EAST

"Phew! It's very hot up here," sighs Timothy, as they fly over the deserts of the Middle East. He looks down at the crowd of camels below. "Why do they have humps?" he asks. "Camels use their humps to store food, so they can travel for long distances in the desert without food or water," says Mr. Mombo. "I wish we could do the same," he laughs, looking at their nearly empty food bag.

How many yellow camels are there?

How many camels are lying down?

Some camels have blankets. Can you count them?

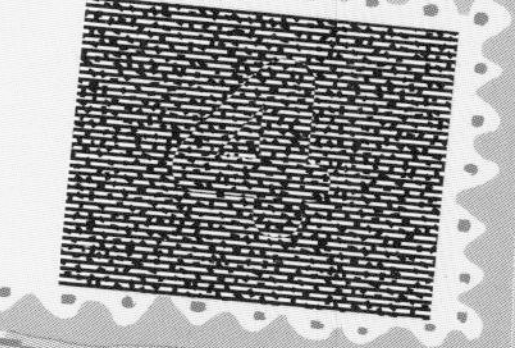

How many palm trees can you see?

CAN YOU SEE?

Can you find the camels holding tails?

Can you see the camel drinking from the pool?

Mr. Mombo has dropped his book. Can you see it?

Can you find the spider?

Where is Mr. Mombo's parrot?